Rob Childs has written over seventy books, mainly aimed at young people. He is a former teacher and has trained at the Dyslexia Institute. He enjoys writing books about sport, particularly football, and science fiction. Rob's best-known books are those in **The Big Match** and **Soccer Mad** series, plus the **Time Rangers** stories about time-travelling footballers.

About Diffusion books

Diffusion publishes books for adults who are emerging readers. There are two series:

Books in the Diamond series are ideally suited to those who are relatively new to reading or who have not practised their reading skills for some time (approximately Entry Level 2 to 3 in adult literacy levels).

Books in the Star series are for those who are ready for the next step. These books will help to build confidence and inspire readers to tackle longer books (approximately Entry Level 3 to Level 1 in adult literacy levels).

Other books available in the Diamond series are:

Snake by Matt Dickinson

Fans by Niall Griffiths

Breaking the Chain by Darren Richards

Lost at Sea by Joel Smith

Uprising by Alex Wheatle

Books available in the Star series are:

Not Such a Bargain by Toby Forward

Barcelona Away by Tom Palmer

Forty-six Quid and a Bag of Dirty Washing by Andy Croft

Bare Freedom by Andy Croft

One Shot by Lena Semaan

Nowhere to Run by Michael Crowley

Space Ark

Rob Childs

First published in Great Britain in 2017

Diffusion
an imprint of SPCK
36 Causton Street
London SW1P 4ST
www.spck.org.uk

ISBN 978–1–908713–11–7
eBook ISBN 978–1–908713–21–6

Typeset by Lapiz Digital Services, Chennai
Printed in Great Britain by Ashford Colour Press
Subsequently digitally reprinted in Great Britain

eBook by Lapiz Digital Services, Chennai

Produced on paper from sustainable forests

Contents

1
Storm

Ben liked collecting butterflies. He had started when he was a boy. His dad used to take him out into the fields near their home and Ben would catch butterflies in his net.

If they caught a good one, they put it in a killing jar. This was just a jam jar with a piece of old rag soaked in ether at the bottom. The ether killed the butterfly without harming its wings.

When they got home, Ben and his dad would stick a pin in the butterfly's body and put the butterfly in a display case.

Ben needed one last butterfly, a Large Copper, and then his set of British butterflies would be complete. He knew that some people thought butterfly collecting was wrong. There were even laws to protect rare butterflies like the Large Copper. But still, he really wanted to complete his set.

Ben's wife, Anne, hated the fact that Ben collected butterflies and killed them. Their ten-year-old son, Jack, hated it too. They both said it was cruel.

Anne and Jack would not usually go out with Ben looking for butterflies but today Ben said that he would take them to the cinema on the way home.

They were out in the middle of a field when it started raining really heavily. Ben, Anne and Jack ran over to some trees to get out of the wet. Suddenly there was a flash of lightning.

'Come on, we can't stay here,' shouted Ben over a loud boom of thunder.

'We will get soaked,' cried Anne. She looked down at Jack, who stood between them. 'Let's wait until the rain stops.'

Ben shook his head.

'It's too risky under the trees,' he called out, and then made a joke of it. 'It's better to be drowned than fried by lightning!'

'Please can we stay here?' said Jack. 'Or we will get too wet to go to the cinema.'

'No, we need to get back to the car as quickly as we can,' Ben said. 'Come on! Let's make a run for it.'

Holding hands, they ran out into the open. But before they had gone twenty metres, they stopped dead in their tracks and looked upwards.

There was a circle of darkness above them that was blacker than any thunderclouds. It was coming lower and lower with a deep humming sound.

The rain stopped as if a giant tap in the sky had been turned off.

'What the hell?' Ben cried.

Suddenly, they were all thrown to the ground by a beam of dazzling blue light. They lay still, with their arms over their eyes to protect them from the bright light.

What do you think?

- What do you think the 'circle of darkness' above the family might be?

- Why do you think Ben still catches butterflies even though his family think it's wrong?

- Why is it important to have laws that help protect wildlife?

2
Space zoo

Ben slowly woke up. There was a disgusting smell. It made him feel sick. He rolled over onto his side and vomited. Then he crawled away from the pile of stinking sick until he bumped into some kind of metal barrier.

'Are those bars?' he wondered. He was still only half awake.

He sat up and leaned back against the bars. His head hurt. It was dark, so he could not see much.

It looked as if he was in a cage. Then he saw Anne curled up in the far corner of the cage. There was no sign of Jack.

Ben could hear lots of grunts, groans and growls coming from outside the cage.

'Where on earth are we?' he said to himself. Then Ben got a real fright. A strange voice spoke back to him!

'You are not on Earth now,' said the voice.

Ben was shocked. Somehow, he knew for sure that whatever had said those words was not human.

'What? Who's that?' he asked.

But before the voice answered, Anne woke up.

'What's that disgusting smell?' she asked.

'I don't know,' Ben told her. 'Are you OK?'

Anne looked around. 'Where's Jack?' she asked.

Ben said, 'I don't know that either, but I'm damn sure I'm going to find out as soon as I can.'

Just then the roof of the cage began to slide open. The cage was filled with dazzling light. Ben covered his eyes, then peeped between his fingers, looking around him.

He could not believe what he saw. There was a row of cages, and in each cage were creatures with strange shapes and faces, furs and coloured skins.

Ben was too shocked to speak.

The two creatures in the cage next to Ben and Anne were tall and thin, with green bodies that seemed slim enough to fit through the bars. The only thing stopping them was their huge heads. And on each head the creatures had eight eyes.

Suddenly, a lot of warm liquid came down from above and swirled around their cages. Anne gave a scream but at that moment one of the alien creatures in the cage next to them flicked its long green tail through the bars and wrapped itself around Anne, holding her above the liquid.

'Hey!' cried Ben. 'Let go of my wife.'

'Do you want her to drown?' asked the alien.

'No, I don't!' Ben said.

The liquid was some kind of cleaning fluid. By now it was draining out of the cage. The alien put Anne gently back down.

'Who are you?' Ben demanded.

'We are Trimlons,' the alien said. *'We are space travellers. We have learned your language.'*

'What's going on here?' Ben asked.

'You were captured and drugged. You are on show, just like us,' explained the Trimlon.

'On show?' Ben repeated. 'What do you mean?'

'This is a space zoo,' said the Trimlon.

What do you think?

- What do you think has happened to Ben and Anne?

- How do you think Ben and Anne feel?

- Do you think there are such things as aliens? Why?

3
Visiting time

Ben gasped. 'A zoo!' he said. 'They can't put us in a zoo. We are human beings, not animals. They have got no right!'

Next they heard a loud noise like an engine starting up and hot air was blasted into the cage. It smelled sickly sweet.

'It's air freshener,' said the Trimlon. *'To hide the smell.'*

'What a terrible place!' said Anne. 'What are we doing here?'

'Well, at least we've got a cage of our own,' Ben said. 'We don't have to share with any of that lot out there.'

The two Trimlons were in the cage on one side of Ben and Anne. On their other side was a large and hairy alien, like a bear. It stared hard at them from one red eye in the middle of its head. It did not look friendly.

In the corner of the room, Ben saw a lift coming down. When the doors opened, two aliens crawled out. They looked like giant caterpillars. Their bodies were about a metre long, and they had black and red stripes on their scales. They had five pairs of legs but the ones at the front were raised and ended in claws.

They wriggled around the huge room, pushing straw bedding into each cage with long-handled brushes. They were careful to stay well back from the teeth and claws of the aliens in the cages. Ben guessed that these caterpillar aliens must be the zoo keepers.

Next, the keepers pushed a bowl of food into each cage.

Anne looked at the grey lumpy stuff in the bowl.

'Yuk!' she said.

'It's all there is to eat,' said Ben. 'I guess it's either eat this or starve.'

'I would rather starve,' Anne said and sat back down against the wall.

Ben did not like to think what the food might be but he was hungry. He took a small bite.

He gagged. It tasted as bad as it looked. He couldn't eat it.

Ben and Anne were both worried about Jack but they felt so sleepy. They were still feeling the effects of the drugs they had been given when they were captured. They sat together in the corner furthest away from the bear-like alien and fell asleep.

When Ben woke up a while later, he rubbed his eyes. At first he had no idea where he was. Then he remembered the awful truth and his heart sank.

He heard more strange noises and he woke Anne up.

'What do you think is going on?' he asked her.

'It looks like it might be visiting time,' Anne said, pointing up.

Ben looked up. Now that the roof was open he could see lots of alien faces looking down at them.

'Most of those *things* up there are so weird they should be in the cages, not us,' Ben said.

One of the Trimlons spoke. *'Not all of them will leave here.'*

'You mean, some of them will end up in the zoo like us?' Ben asked.

The other Trimlon nodded its enormous head and said, *'Yes, we are bait. This is also how the zoo gets its food.'*

'Food?' Ben asked. 'What do you mean?'

'Not all of those taken will be put on show in the zoo,' said the Trimlon. *'Some of them will be eaten.'*

Ben was now even more afraid for Jack. He could only pray that he was OK.

'Do you have any idea where we are?' he asked the Trimlon.

'Maybe the space zoo has docked at a space station,' said the Trimlon. *'The space zoo is very popular. It travels all over the galaxy.'*

Ben and Anne looked up at the alien visitors staring down at them. Some of them pointed down at the cages and laughed.

'I tell you what,' Anne said. 'I'm never going to a zoo again.'

Ben remembered how he had laughed and pointed at monkeys in the zoo. Maybe the monkeys hadn't found it so funny.

'Huh! Fat chance of that, anyway,' he muttered. 'We are stuck here, at least until we end up as grub!'

What do you think?

- What do you think might have happened to Jack? How do you think Ben and Anne feel about Jack?

- What are some good ways to help someone you are worried about?

- How does Ben feel about zoos now that he is in one? What's good and bad about zoos?

4

The Masters

'Where can Jack be?' said Anne.

She kept asking the same question, but Ben could not answer.

'Look, I'm sure he's OK,' Ben said again. 'Maybe they keep the young ones in a separate part of the zoo, that's all.'

'If only we knew for sure,' said Anne, her eyes full of tears. 'Maybe we will never see him again.'

'Of course we will,' Ben said. 'It will just be a matter of time.'

Ben looked across at the ugly, one-eyed bear in the cage next to them. It had many legs with sharp claws. Suddenly one of the legs shot out and clanged against the bars, making Ben jump back in alarm.

'We had best keep well away from that one,' he said.

'You are right. It is not friendly,' one of the Trimlons said.

'What the hell is it?' asked Ben.

'We do not know,' said the Trimlon. *'It does not speak.'*

'How can you stand it in this place?' said Ben. 'Have you tried to escape?'

The other Trimlon shook its great head and said, *'We have not had a chance, until you came.'*

'What difference do we make?' asked Ben.

'We can work together,' said the first Trimlon. *'The Masters have made a big mistake putting humans next to Trimlons.'*

'Those creatures are not our masters!' shouted Ben. 'They are just big stupid caterpillars, that's all they are.'

'Yes,' said the first Trimlon, *'but think what caterpillars become.'*

'They become butterflies,' said Ben. 'Are you trying to tell us that butterflies are in charge of the space zoo? On Earth, butterflies are just pretty little insects. I've collected them since I was a boy.'

'And here the butterflies are the Masters, and now they have collected you for their zoo,' said the second Trimlon.

Anne gave Ben a hard look and he quickly changed the subject.

'Do you have any idea where our son might be?' he asked.

The Trimlons shook their large heads.

'He might be in another part of the space ship,' said the first Trimlon. 'We will ask all the Trimlons on board if they have seen him.'

'How will you do that?' asked Ben.

'Think-power,' said the Trimlon. 'We can think to one another.'

'It must be some kind of mind-reading,' Anne said.

Some time later, the visitors left and the roof closed again, shutting out the bright light.

Ben took his chance to ask the Trimlons more questions. He learned that the caterpillars were the slaves of the Masters and were used as either keepers or guards.

Only the very best caterpillars were allowed to make a cocoon and transform into a galactic butterfly, becoming one of the Masters.

There was still no news of Jack. None of the Trimlons on the ship had seen a human child.

'He must be in the food store,' said the Trimlon.

'Do you think he might be dead?' Ben asked.

'The Masters might have drugged him,' said the Trimlon. 'They like to drink warm blood, so they freeze their food and then bring it back to life when they are ready to eat it.'

When Anne heard this, she burst into tears. Ben put an arm around her shoulders.

'It will be OK,' he told her. 'Jack won't end up as grub for these monsters.'

Ben turned and spoke again to the Trimlons. 'We are going to get out of here and we will free all the aliens being held in the zoo. Well, maybe not the angry bear. It looks too dangerous.'

'The bear could be useful. We may need it,' said the Trimlon.

Ben, Anne and the two Trimlons thought about how they could escape. They had lots of ideas.

They finally came up with a plan. With luck it might just work. By now, Ben was so frightened for Jack that he was ready to try anything.

'If Jack has been frozen, we don't have much time. We have to act quickly,' said Ben. 'We will put our plan into action at the next feeding time.'

What do you think?

- What would be good about being able to read other people's minds? How would you feel if other people could read your mind?

- The Trimlons' ability to mind-read may have helped them to cope with being locked up. What would be some other good ways of coping with losing your freedom?

- The Trimlon tells Ben, *'We can work together.'* Do you prefer to work by yourself or in a team? Why?

5
Escape

'Help!' shouted Ben. 'She's dead!' He waved
his arms through the bars to get the keeper's
attention. 'My wife is dead!'

Anne was very good at playing dead. She lay
still against the side of the cage nearest to the
Trimlons. She had smeared blood across her face.
The blood was real. She had got it by gashing
her knee against the bars. She was ready to do
anything to save her son.

'Dead!' Ben cried again.

All the cage doors were controlled from a panel in the centre of the room. The plan was to trick one of the keepers into opening Ben and Anne's door and coming into their cage. It was an old trick but Ben hoped the caterpillars would fall for it.

A caterpillar finally crawled over to their cage to check what all the noise was about. It looked in but then it seemed to lose interest and it moved away.

Their escape plan had failed before it had even started!

But then the giant caterpillar came back with a brush and stood outside the cage door. The other keeper opened the door from the control panel and then quickly wriggled over to their cage.

'It looks like I might have to deal with one of these monsters myself,' thought Ben.

The first caterpillar came into the cage and pushed Ben away with the brush. The second caterpillar wriggled into the cage to drag out Anne's body. That was when the Trimlons struck.

They flicked their tails through the bars and wrapped them around the front and back ends of the second keeper, pinning it against the bars to make it let go of Anne.

At the same time Ben jumped at the second keeper with a rugby-style tackle. The keeper was surprised by the attack and it fell back onto the floor of the cage.

Ben fought with the giant caterpillar, but it was very strong. It was only about half Ben's size, but it had sharp claws and teeth that were used for tearing and chewing flesh. Ben felt hopeless. He knew he would lose this fight.

The caterpillar wrapped itself around Ben and squeezed the air from his lungs. Ben could not breathe. His chest was nearly crushed. Then, all of a sudden, he felt the caterpillar let go of him.

Ben saw Anne standing over the caterpillar holding the heavy brush.

'I gave it a great smack with this thing!' she cried.

'Great stuff!' he laughed, giving her a hug. 'Well done!'

'Go quickly!' said one of the Trimlons. *'Go and open all the doors.'*

Ben ran to the control panel, but didn't know which buttons to press. He tried one, and a cage door slid open nearby. Two large blue lizard-like aliens ran out.

'We can't just let them all out,' shouted Anne. 'We don't know which ones we can trust. We might end up being their dinner!'

Ben looked over to the bear-like alien, which was shaking the bars of its cage and howling.

'We just have to risk it,' yelled Ben. 'We have no choice.'

Ben began to jab at the buttons, and more cage doors opened. Just then, the other keeper got away from the Trimlons' grip by biting off one of their tails. The Trimlon gave a howl of pain as the keeper charged at Ben.

The keeper had not seen the bear, which was now out of its cage.

The starving bear jumped on the caterpillar and tore it in half. Then it started to eat it.

'Enjoy your dinner,' cried Ben.

What do you think?

- Anne says of the aliens in the cages, 'We don't know which ones we can trust.' Do you find it hard to trust someone you don't know? How might they earn your trust?

- Do you think other people can trust you? Why or why not?

- Ben says, 'We have no choice.' What does it feel like to have no choice? Or do we always have choices?

- If you had been hungry for a long time, what would your first meal be?

6

Aliens united

Other aliens began to come out of their cages. A few fights broke out between them. Perhaps they had been sizing one another up for weeks, or even months.

Alarm bells began to ring and caterpillar guards ran in. They did not last long. They were set upon by many large aliens, including the hungry bear.

The Trimlons took charge of the situation. They sorted out the fights between the aliens and somehow convinced them to work together.

Together, Ben and the Trimlons were able to work the lift. Some of the aliens went up in the lift to the viewing platform. Some of them even flew or climbed up the walls themselves.

Then the aliens got into the other rooms of the space zoo and set free more captives, including other Trimlons. They would need all the help they could get in the battle to come.

Ben and Anne looked out for any sign of Jack.

'He's *got* to be here somewhere,' Anne cried.

'We will just have to keep looking until we find him,' Ben told her. 'The Trimlons said he might be in the food store. Let's search for that.'

But just then some armed caterpillar guards arrived. They were bigger than the keepers and held laser guns in their front claws. They fired at anything in their way with deadly beams of light.

The aliens were desperate for their freedom so they fought bravely. A few of them died, but the caterpillar guards were outnumbered.

The bear did most of the damage. It was so angry that it went crazy, killing many of the guards.

The guards saw that the bear was their biggest problem. Together they turned their weapons on it until it fell dead with a last great roar.

There were now over a hundred different types of alien roaming the space ship. Some of them carried the guards' weapons and together they were a mighty force.

It was not until they were deep into the heart of the ship that Ben and Anne first saw one of the Masters. The galactic butterfly was a truly amazing sight.

The giant insect's body was about the size of a human. It had four huge wings, covered in brightly coloured scales. As the wings flapped they blocked the passageway, so the aliens could not go forward.

The Master squirted jets of liquid over the first few aliens. Their skin began to burn and they rolled on the floor in agony.

'*Acid!*' cried a Trimlon. '*Keep back!*'

The Master came towards them but when it saw that many of its enemies were armed it stopped in its tracks.

A Trimlon turned a laser gun on to full power and fired. The Master was blown to pieces and its scales burst into the air like confetti.

What do you think?

- The Trimlons take charge of the situation and lead the alien forces. What do you think makes a good leader?

- Why was Ben right to let the one-eyed bear out of its cage? Do you feel sorry for it, or not? Why?

- Why do the freed aliens stop fighting among themselves? What are some good ways to cope with living or working with people you don't like?

7
Cocoon

Ben and Anne kept away from the fighting. Humans seemed weak compared with the aliens and there was little they could do to help. They also had to stay alive to rescue Jack.

Even so, when he got the chance Ben picked up one of the guards' laser guns.

'What have you got that thing for?' said Anne. 'You don't even know how to use it.'

'I hope I won't have to,' replied Ben.

'But I guess I just press this thing that looks like a trigger.'

'Don't point it at me!' Anne cried, pushing his arm away.

'Sorry,' Ben said. 'I didn't mean to.'

'You should give it to somebody else,' said Anne.

Ben shook his head and tucked the gun into the belt of his jeans.

'No, I'll keep it,' he said. 'Just in case.'

As they went round the next corner, they saw what the Master had been guarding. Through large windows they could see rows and rows of what looked like cocoons hanging from racks.

'This must be where the caterpillars go to change into butterflies,' Anne said.

'Maybe,' Ben said. 'But it might even be their food store.'

'Do you think this is where Jack is?' she asked.

'That's what we are going to find out,' Ben told her. 'We are not going anywhere until we've taken a good look around in there.'

By now the fighting had moved on but the Trimlons had left two armed aliens to act as bodyguards for Ben and Anne. The door into the room of cocoons would not open, so one of the bodyguards blasted a hole through it.

Ben and Anne stepped inside.

'It's like walking into a freezer!' Anne said, and she shivered in the cold.

'That's probably just what it is,' said Ben, nodding. 'Come on, let's look and see if Jack is in here.'

Most of the cocoons were black with age, and it was impossible to tell what might be inside.

Some looked as if they had been spun more recently and the silky cases were still clear.

Anne suddenly let out a loud cry. 'Jack!'

Ben rushed towards a cocoon with Jack's body inside.

He swallowed hard. It was not a pretty sight. Jack's face was deathly white.

'The Trimlons said he's probably just in a drugged sleep,' Ben told Anne. 'You know, in a kind of coma.'

Anne's face was almost as pale as Jack's.

'Let's hope they are right,' she said.

'Come on, we must get him out of this cocoon while we have the chance,' Ben told her. 'You hold it to stop it falling while I try to break it open.'

Ben reached up to Jack's chest and tore at the cocoon with his bare hands. The silky material was very strong. Ben had to use all his strength to rip it apart. As the material tore, Jack fell forward into his arms. The boy's body felt cold and damp, but he was still breathing.

'He's alive!' cried Ben. 'Let's put him on the floor and get rid of all this stuff sticking to him. Then we must get him out of this cold room.'

They pulled away all the strands of the cocoon from their son's face and body. Then they tried to rub some life back into him. Jack did not wake up.

Ben looked at his son's limp body and shook his head.

'Let's hope the Trimlons know how to get him out of this coma,' he said.

Anne sat down and hugged Jack tightly to try to warm him. She talked to him softly in the hope that he might be able to hear her.

Ben went over to where the bodyguard aliens were standing. They could not see anything, but sounds of battle were coming from somewhere nearby.

Ben took the gun out of his belt and looked at it closely to check how it might be fired. He did not dare try it out. He hoped he would not have to use it. He turned and walked back to Anne.

'What's going on out there?' she asked.

'I can't see anything,' said Ben, 'but I could hear some shooting. Maybe I should go to see what is happening.'

'It's cold in here but at least we are away from the fighting,' Anne said. 'Please stay here with us. We need to be together.'

Ben put his arms around them both and held them tightly.

'I expect it will all soon be over,' he said. 'One way or another.'

What do you think?

- Should Ben give the gun to someone else or keep it? Why?

- Do you think Ben should stay with Anne and Jack or go to join the battle? Why?

- What is the difference between choosing to stay out of a fight and being a coward?

8
Dead and gone

The fight between the aliens and the caterpillar guards was going on all over the space ship.

Anne hid behind a crate, holding Jack in her arms.

Ben kept on the alert. It was a good job that he did so.

One of the Masters fought its way towards the food store with a group of caterpillars. The two bodyguards did their best and shot the caterpillars dead but somehow the Master got through.

The Master went into the food store and began to spray acid onto the hanging bodies in the cocoons. It was so angry that it wanted to kill all the frozen victims.

Ben could not hide and watch the defenceless aliens be killed in their cocoons. He took a deep breath, then stood up, holding the gun in both his shaking hands.

'Die!' he cried, and squeezed the trigger as hard as he could.

Ben was lucky. His aim was good and the Master vanished from view.

'Got it!' shouted Ben. 'I blew it to bits!'

'Well done, but you shouldn't have put yourself in such danger,' Anne said. 'Your son needs you. And so do I.'

'I couldn't just watch and do nothing, and he might have turned on us next,' Ben said.

Ben stayed with Anne and Jack. He didn't know if any more Masters or guards would try to return to the food store.

The fighting went on for hours. In the end, most of the guards were killed. Their guns were taken and used by the aliens. Some of the aliens lost their lives in the fighting, including the Trimlon whose tail had been bitten off when they first escaped from the cage. Without a tail, it was not strong enough to fight for long and it died protecting a group of alien children.

Some of the Masters tried to save themselves by hiding in quiet parts of the ship, but the aliens soon found them and took their revenge. The Masters were shown no mercy at all.

They had to be killed before they could spray their acid. They were too dangerous to take alive.

Then Ben and Anne heard a voice calling out to them. It had to be a Trimlon.

'We are here,' Ben cried, showing himself. 'We are safe.'

At least Ben hoped that was the case. He was still holding the gun, but had promised Anne that he would soon give it to one of the aliens.

'Yes, you are safe now,' the Trimlon told them. *'We all are.'*

'Are you sure?' asked Anne.

The Trimlon nodded its huge head. *'The Masters are dead and the guards are locked in their own cages. You are free to come out.'*

'We need a doctor for our son,' said Anne.

'I will find someone who can help him,' the Trimlon promised. *'Follow me.'*

The Trimlon found an alien doctor and soon Jack was getting help. Ben and Anne watched as the doctor went to work on their son.

At last Jack opened his eyes. When he saw his parents, he gave a weak smile.

'You are going to be OK,' Ben told him. 'You are in good hands now. Well, if you can call those strange things *hands.*'

What do you think?

- Was Anne right to say to Ben, 'You shouldn't have put yourself in such danger'? What do you think about what he did?

- Have you ever stuck up for someone who could not defend themselves? How did it make you feel? How do you think it made them feel?

- Who or what do you think would be worth fighting for?

9
Homeward bound

The space ship was now under the command of the Trimlons. Some of the other aliens also knew how to fly it. They set off through the stars to return all the aliens to their own worlds.

It would be some time before they reached Earth.

Jack made a full recovery and soon felt normal again. The family spent a lot of time together, looking out of the ship's windows.

'Do you think we will ever get home?' Jack asked.

'Of course,' Ben told him. 'But for now we should just enjoy the view.'

They watched as they flew past stars and planets.

Jack kept saying, 'It's totally awesome.'

Ben and Anne agreed.

Jack found some paper and pens, and began to draw some of the sights. He was a good artist and his pictures were excellent. He also drew a Trimlon, a few of the aliens and even one of the caterpillars.

'We might be able to sell some of these when we get back,' Ben said as a joke. 'You will become rich and famous!'

'No way!' Jack laughed. 'I will just put them up on my bedroom wall.'

'You'll be famous, anyway,' Ben told him. 'You know, after all this. The whole world will want to hear your story.'

'You can tell it,' Jack said. 'I was asleep most of the time.'

'Yes, and it's just as well you didn't start growing butterfly wings in that sack,' Ben said.

Jack grinned and said, 'Wings might be quite useful. I could have flown to school!'

'Save you being late as usual,' Ben said with a smile. 'The other kids would have been green with envy when you landed in the playground.'

'One of the doctors was green, like the Trimlons,' Anne said. 'In fact, the aliens were all different colours.'

'Colour doesn't matter,' said Ben. 'What matters is whether they are the kind of alien that captures someone and puts them on display, or the kind of alien that helps others and fights for freedom.'

Anne and Jack both gave Ben a hard look.

'What?' asked Ben, looking puzzled.

'It's just like you and the butterflies,' said Jack. 'You trap them and kill them for your collection.'

'Yes,' agreed Anne. 'Now you know what it feels like to be captured and put on show. Maybe now you'll finally stop collecting butterflies.'

'I will never do it again,' Ben promised. 'And I will throw the collection away as soon as we get back home.'

'I'm very glad to hear you say that,' said Anne.

'Well, I don't think any of us will want to see another creature kept locked up ever again,' Ben said. 'Dead or alive!'

'Or perhaps even just asleep,' added Jack with a smile.

What do you think?

- Do you think anyone will believe Ben's story when he gets back to Earth? Why?

- What does Ben mean when he says, 'Colour doesn't matter'? Is he right? Why, or why not?

- Have you seen anything in nature that left you feeling amazed? What's the most awe-inspiring thing you've ever seen?

Books available in the Diamond series

Space Ark
by Rob Childs (ISBN: 978 1 908713 11 7)
Ben and his family are walking in the woods when they are thrown to the ground by a dazzling light. Ben wakes up to find they have been abducted by aliens. Will Ben be able to defeat the aliens and save his family before it is too late?

Snake
by Matt Dickinson (ISBN: 978 1 908713 12 4)
Liam loves visiting the local pet shop and is desperate to have his own pet snake. Then one day, Mr Nash, the owner of the shop, just disappears. What has happened to Mr Nash? And how far will Liam go to get what he wants?

Fans
by Niall Griffiths (ISBN: 978 1 908713 13 1)
Jerry is excited about taking his young son Stevie to watch the big match. But when trouble breaks out between the fans, Jerry and Stevie can't escape the shouting, fighting and flying glass. And then Stevie gets lost in the crowd. What will Jerry do next? And what will happen to Stevie?

Breaking the Chain

by Darren Richards (ISBN: 978 1 908713 08 7)

Ken had a happy life. But then he found out a secret that changed everything. Now he is in prison for murder. Then Ken meets the new lad on the wing, Josh. Why does Ken tell Josh his secret? And could it be the key to their freedom?

Lost at Sea

by Joel Smith (ISBN: 978 1 908713 09 4)

Alec loves his job in the Royal Navy. His new mission is to save refugees from unsafe boats. But when a daring rescue attempt goes wrong, Alec is the one who needs saving. Who will come to help him?

Uprising: A true story

by Alex Wheatle (ISBN 978 1 908713 10 0)

Alex had a tough start in life. He grew up in care until he was fourteen, when he was sent to live in a hostel in Brixton. After being sent to prison for taking part in the Brixton riots, Alex's future seemed hopeless. But then something happened to change his life…

You can order these books by writing to Diffusion, SPCK, 36 Causton Street, London SW1P 4ST or visiting www.spck.org.uk/what-we-do/prison-fiction/